Rumpelstiltskin

First published in 2008 by
Franklin Watts
338 Euston Road
London
NW1 3BH

Franklin Watts Australia
Level 17/207 Kent Street
Sydney
NSW 2000

A CIP catalogue record for this book is available from the British Library.

ISBN 978 0 7496 7902 6 (hbk)
ISBN 978 0 7496 7908 8 (pbk)

Series Editor: Melanie Palmer
Series Advisor: Dr Barrie Wade
Series Designer: Peter Scoulding

Printed in China

Franklin Watts is a division of
Hachette Children's Books,
an Hachette Livre UK company.

Rumpelstiltskin

by Anne Walter and Peter Cottrill

Once upon a time, a poor, foolish miller lived with his daughter.

The miller wanted to please the king. So, one day, he took his daughter to the king's palace.

"My girl can spin straw into gold," the miller lied, boastfully. The king was pleased. He loved gold.

The king took the girl to a room full of straw. "Spin this into gold by morning, or you will die!" he ordered, locking the door.

The girl started to cry. She had no idea how to spin straw into gold, or how to spin anything!

Then a funny little man appeared.
"What's the matter?" he asked.
"I must spin all this straw into gold," the girl told him.

"If I help you, what will you give me?" asked the little man, smiling. "Take my necklace," she replied.

The little man took the necklace and sat at the spinning wheel until all the straw had been turned into gold. Then he vanished.

When the king saw the gold, he was amazed. But he wanted more.

The king took the girl to a bigger room with even more straw.
"Now spin all this straw into gold," he ordered, locking the door again.
Once more, the girl started to cry.

Then the funny little man returned.
"If I help you, what will you give me this time?" he asked.
"Take my ring," she replied.

Again, the man spun the straw until the room gleamed with gold. Then he vanished.

When the king saw the gold, he was delighted, but he wanted more.

The king took the girl to a huge room, bursting with straw. “Spin this straw into gold, and I will make you my queen,” he promised.

As the girl wept, the little man returned. “I will help you, but what will you give me?” he asked. The girl had nothing left.

"After you become queen, you will give me your first child," he told her. Then he spun all the straw into gold.

The king kept his promise and made the girl his queen. Later, she had a beautiful baby boy.

Then the little man came back for his reward. "I will have your child, just as you promised," he said.

"Oh please don't take my child," sobbed the queen.

The man felt sorry for the queen. "Let's play a game," he said. "If you can guess my name, you can keep your child. You have three days."

On the first day, the queen guessed:

"Is it Roger or Peter?

Barry or Harry?"

"No! None of them," laughed the little man. "Two days left!" he said and skipped away.

On the second day, the queen tried stranger names. “Is it Rumbleweed, Twistybeard, or Cleverchops?”

"No, No, No!" he laughed again.
"One day left," he said and
vanished.

The queen needed help, so she sent out some spies. Deep in the forest, they heard a little man singing.

“Ha, ha, the queen will never win,
She’ll never guess I’m ...
Rumpelstiltskin!”

On the third day, the queen said:
"Hello ... Rumpelstiltskin!"
The little man was so shocked
he could not speak.

He stamped his feet and bit his hat,
then disappeared and that was that!

Hopscotch has been specially designed to fit the requirements of the Literacy Framework. It offers real books by top authors and illustrators for children developing their reading skills. There are 55 Hopscotch stories to choose from:

Marvin, the Blue Pig
ISBN 978 0 7496 4619 6

Plip and Plop
ISBN 978 0 7496 4620 2

The Queen's Dragon
ISBN 978 0 7496 4618 9

Flora McQuack
ISBN 978 0 7496 4621 9

Willie the Whale
ISBN 978 0 7496 4623 3

Naughty Nancy
ISBN 978 0 7496 4622 6

Run!
ISBN 978 0 7496 4705 6

The Playground Snake
ISBN 978 0 7496 4706 3

"Sausages!"
ISBN 978 0 7496 4707 0

Bear in Town
ISBN 978 0 7496 5875 5

Pippin's Big Jump
ISBN 978 0 7496 4710 0

Whose Birthday Is It?
ISBN 978 0 7496 4709 4

The Princess and the Frog
ISBN 978 0 7496 5129 9

Flynn Flies High
ISBN 978 0 7496 5130 5

Clever Cat
ISBN 978 0 7496 5131 2

Moo!
ISBN 978 0 7496 5332 3

Izzie's Idea
ISBN 978 0 7496 5334 7

Roly-poly Rice Ball
ISBN 978 0 7496 5333 0

I Can't Stand It!
ISBN 978 0 7496 5765 9

Cockerel's Big Egg
ISBN 978 0 7496 5767 3

How to Teach a Dragon Manners
ISBN 978 0 7496 5873 1

The Truth about those Billy Goats
ISBN 978 0 7496 5766 6

Marlowe's Mum and the Tree House
ISBN 978 0 7496 5874 8

The Truth about Hansel and Gretel
ISBN 978 0 7496 4708 7

The Best Den Ever
ISBN 978 0 7496 5876 2

ADVENTURE STORIES

Aladdin and the Lamp
ISBN 978 0 7496 6692 7

Blackbeard the Pirate
ISBN 978 0 7496 6690 3

George and the Dragon
ISBN 978 0 7496 6691 0

Jack the Giant-Killer
ISBN 978 0 7496 6693 4

TALES OF KING ARTHUR

1. The Sword in the Stone
ISBN 978 0 7496 6694 1

2. Arthur the King
ISBN 978 0 7496 6695 8

3. The Round Table
ISBN 978 0 7496 6697 2

4. Sir Lancelot and the Ice Castle
ISBN 978 0 7496 6698 9

TALES OF ROBIN HOOD

Robin and the Knight
ISBN 978 0 7496 6699 6

Robin and the Monk
ISBN 978 0 7496 6700 9

Robin and the Silver Arrow
ISBN 978 0 7496 6703 0

Robin and the Friar
ISBN 978 0 7496 6702 3

FAIRY TALES

The Emperor's New Clothes
ISBN 978 0 7496 7421 2

Cinderella
ISBN 978 0 7496 7417 5

Snow White
ISBN 978 0 7496 7418 2

Jack and the Beanstalk
ISBN 978 0 7496 7422 9

The Three Billy Goats Gruff
ISBN 978 0 7496 7420 5

The Pied Piper of Hamelin
ISBN 978 0 7496 7419 9

Goldilocks and the Three Bears
ISBN 978 0 7496 7897 5 *
ISBN 978 0 7496 7903 3

Hansel and Gretel
ISBN 978 0 7496 7898 2 *
ISBN 978 0 7496 7904 0

The Three Little Pigs
ISBN 978 0 7496 7899 9 *
ISBN 978 0 7496 7905 7

Rapunzel
ISBN 978 0 7496 7900 2 *
ISBN 978 0 7496 7906 4

Little Red Riding Hood
ISBN 978 0 7496 7901 9 *
ISBN 978 0 7496 7907 1

Rumpelstiltskin
ISBN 978 0 7496 7902 6*
ISBN 978 0 7496 7908 8

HISTORIES

Toby and the Great Fire of London
ISBN 978 0 7496 7410 6

Pocahontas the Peacemaker
ISBN 978 0 7496 7411 3

Grandma's Seaside Bloomers
ISBN 978 0 7496 7412 0

Hoorah for Mary Seacole
ISBN 978 0 7496 7413 7

Remember the 5th of November
ISBN 978 0 7496 7414 4

Tutankhamun and the Golden Chariot
ISBN 978 0 7496 7415 1

*** hardback**